THE EXCHANGE STUDENT

MALCOLM IN THE MIDDLE

THE EXCHANGE STUDENT

BY PAM POLLACK & MEG BELVISO

SCHOLASTIC INC.

New York   Toronto   London   Auckland   Sydney
Mexico City   New Delhi   Hong Kong

THE EXCHANGE STUDENT

Nothing ever changes in our house. Every day my brother Reese elbows me in the ribs on the way to the bathroom. Then my little brother Dewey tells me about some dream he had where a monster came into our room and went through his underwear drawer. Then my mom yells for us all to come down to breakfast and tells us there's no Pop-Tarts – again. Then my dad looks all over the house for his car keys and finds them in his pocket. If I'm lucky my brother Francis calls from military school and he's not in trouble. And me? I'm Malcolm. I'm in the middle. It's a pretty good place to be when things are going down. I can usually see what's coming and duck. And there's worse families that you could find yourself in the middle of.

There must be. Somewhere.

CHAPTER ONE

"**D**ewey, get your fingers out of your milk," my mom said, putting a toaster waffle on my brother Reese's plate.

Reese grabbed the maple syrup and squeezed until it burped. Then he put it back down on the table, which was piled with sticky plates, knives, and forks, a pitcher of orange juice, cups, and a football.

Let me show you something. I'm going to take a waffle and put it on the empty plate in the middle of the table. First Reese will call it. Then Dewey will claim he's contaminated it somehow. Mom will yell at them and Dad will get the waffle. Watch.

"It's mine!" says Reese.

"I already spit on it!" says Dewey.

"Will you two stop arguing?!" yells Mom.

And Dad's already eating the waffle without even noticing them.

Isn't that cool? It's like I made all that happen. I'm controlling everything and no one knows it.

"So Malcolm, what are you doing today in your genius class?"

Okay, my mom has asked me that every morning since I was put into the Krelboyne class for smart kids. "Nothing," I said, rolling my eyes. Mom looked at me really closely. She has this power. Like a superhero? When she gives me that look I just open my mouth and start talking. "Okay, we're doing this exchange program," I said. "My teacher thinks we need to meet other kids as weird as we are. We're all supposed to ask if this exchange student can stay with us. But don't feel bad for saying no," I added. I don't get it. How does she always make me do this?

My dad looked up from his paper. "Exchange student?" he repeated, blinking at me like he'd just noticed I was there. "Honey, wasn't I an exchange student? Didn't I live with a Dutch family?"

"Pennsylvania Dutch," Mom said. "You spent a week in Amish Country but they wouldn't let you roller-skate. They said it frightened the horses."

"Right," said Dad. He straightened his tie in the collar of his white, short-sleeved shirt and went back to his paper. All of a sudden my mom got this funny look on her face. I saw a glint in her eyes that I didn't like.

"Mom?" I said. "What is it?"

"You know," said Mom, starting to smile. "That could be fun."

Did she just say what I thought she said? "What?!" I asked her.

Reese started to laugh, spraying chewed-up waffle at me. He wiped his mouth on the sleeve of his blue sweatshirt. "A Krelboyne from another planet? Here? You've got to be kidding!"

"Yeah, she's kidding," I said quickly. "You're kidding, right, Mom?"

But Mom's smile got bigger and bigger. My heart started to beat faster. This couldn't be happening.

"Freak for a week!" Reese announced suddenly. Dewey's eyes darted from me to Reese to Mom. His ears stuck out on the sides of his head like satellite dishes.

"He's not a freak, mister," Mom said sharply, pointing her fork at Reese. "He is just like your brother Malcolm."

Reese grinned at me. I could see the syrup on his chin. My mom was about to ruin my life, but I couldn't think of anything to do about it.

"And he's probably never had a normal family," Mom went on. "For all we know this kid might have been raised in a plastic bubble his whole life."

"There's this kid in my class," said Dewey. "He lives in a bubble. And once he rolled down a hill and he popped."

"No, he didn't," said Reese.

Dad looked up from his paper again. "An exchange student," he said like he was hearing it for the first time. "That could be something."

"I'm going to call the school and say we'll do it," said Mom.

"But . . . but . . . " I began.

"Now listen, you guys," Mom said. "When this boy gets here, no matter how weird he is, you are going to treat him like a member of this family. Just like we treat Malcolm."

Mom gave me a quick smile like she'd said something nice and then ran out of the kitchen to get ready for work. A second later she popped her head back in. "And don't forget," she said. "Malcolm and Reese, I made you appointments to get your hair cut this weekend."

Reese ran a hand through his spiky brown hair and snorted. "Whatever."

Dewey smiled. His hair was still growing out from when he cut it himself under the kitchen table.

When Mom disappeared again Dad leaned in conspiratorially.

"I hope everybody remembers that Mother's Day is coming up," he said. "I think after last year we can rule out cooking Mom breakfast in bed."

"It wasn't my fault," said Reese. "How was I supposed to know pancake syrup could catch on fire?"

"I've never seen eggs explode before," I said, remembering last Mother's Day. We still had singe marks on the ceiling. "It was pretty cool."

"Yes, it was," Dad agreed with me. "But this year we're going out to dinner and you boys are going to have a really nice present for your mom." I wasn't worried about Mother's Day. I'd been through it every year since I was born. It usually ended up with something blowing up and then Mom said she loved us anyway. No problem.

Dewey went to his book bag and pulled out a big

piece of paper with macaroni stuck to it. It was covered in gold glitter.

"What is it?" I asked.

"It's Macaroni Mom," said Dewey.

Of course.

Dad inspected the portrait.

"Excellent likeness, son," he said. He turned back to me and Reese. "You guys better get cracking."

It was Reese's turn to walk Dewey to school. I hitched my backpack onto one shoulder and pushed my hair out of my eyes. As I walked down our street alone, I thought about the mess I'd somehow gotten myself into. "Okay," I said to myself. "What are the chances that this kid is really going to come stay with us? With the reputation my family has, just for insurance purposes, the school is not going to let anyone into my house. Besides, all the parents are probably fighting over who gets to have another genius kid in their house. There's no way my family's even in the running."

I got to the schoolyard and climbed into the trailer next to the tetherball court. That's where my special class has school. The trailer is filled with educational stuff. There's a model of the universe, an ant farm, a skeleton, a fossil bed, lots of computers, and a half-finished model of the *Titanic* made out of Legos. We hadn't worked on it since we all got into a fight about the exact number of rivets that popped out of the side when it hit the iceberg. On the blackboard there was a really long math problem that I won't even bother trying to explain. The teacher was giving everyone a week to solve it. She did this every week and every week I ended up solving it. I didn't want to, but I couldn't help it.

I sat down next to my friend Stevie Kenarban. Stevie moved his wheelchair over to give me some room.

"Hey Stevie," I said. I was still thinking about the exchange student.

"Hi . . . Malcolm . . . What's . . . up?" It takes Stevie a while to say what he wants to say because he always runs out of breath between the words. I didn't have time to answer him, because our teacher came into the trailer. She was carrying an armful of heavy books with papers sticking out of them. She dumped the books on her desk and stood up to make an announcement.

"Okay, class," she said. "I've got some news about our exchange student."

"She looks nervous," I whispered to Stevie.

"She . . . always . . . looks . . . nervous," Stevie whispered back.

"I was hoping that more families would be able to participate in our exchange program," she said. "I didn't realize so many of you come from homes that are climate-controlled for only the number of people in your families. Only one family was able to volunteer for the program."

One family? I poked Stevie. "Please tell me that your family offered to take this kid," I said.

"Are . . . you . . . kidding?" Stevie said. "My . . . parents . . . let . . . a . . . stranger . . . in . . . the . . . house?"

It was a crazy idea. I'd been to Stevie's house and his parents freaked out when there was an extra Cheerio in the box. An extra kid would destroy them.

"Malcolm's family has been kind enough to open their . . . " The teacher looked at me fearfully. ". . . colorful home to our visitor. I'm sure this will work out just fine, really I am," she went on. "Malcolm, could you see me after class? I have a list of emergency numbers I want to give you. Police, fire department, poison control hotline . . ."

"It's 555-1946," I said, rattling off the poison control number. I'd dialed it a million times.

Stevie looked at me with surprise.

"To my brother Dewey, everything looks like candy," I explained.

The teacher gave a little squeak of fear and clutched her emergency numbers.

At lunchtime Stevie and I sat at a table away from the other kids.

"This is unbelievable," I said, poking at whatever was on my plate. The menu said Chili-Mac Surprise, but that could mean almost anything. "The last thing I need is another brother."

"Could . . . be . . . fun," said Stevie.

I frowned at him. "Fun?" I said. "What's fun about it? Do you know how long it's taken me to figure out

exactly how my family works? I had everything going great and then Dewey was born. Adding another player to the board changed the equation
completely. Now I'm going to have to do the math all
over again. "

"I . . . rule . . . my . . . house . . . with . . . an . . .
iron . . . fist," said Stevie.

Yeah, right. He has a bedtime of 8:30.

CHAPTER TWO

The next day was Saturday, which meant cartoons on TV, breakfast on the couch, and me, Reese, and Dewey in our underwear until noon. Okay, this Saturday was Exchange Student Day, but we had like three hours before the teacher brought him over. I threw myself down on the couch and knocked Reese's foot down off the coffee table, barely missing the pile of toy cars Dewey had left on it.

Reese kicked me and kept watching TV. When a commercial came on, Reese turned to me and Dewey, who was sitting next to me in his Mega-Man underwear.

"I've been thinking," Reese said.

Dewey and I stared at each other in shock. Thinking wasn't something Reese usually did.

"You have?" I said.

"Yeah," said Reese, adjusting the elastic on his boxer shorts. "If this kid is staying with us, he can be our slave for the week."

I could feel my eyes get wide. I could see it now: My family gets arrested for enslaving an exchange student. It's all over the news. I'm a bigger freak than ever. "A slave?" I said. "Reese, this is the twenty-first century. There are laws against that."

"Malcolm?" said Dewey, tapping me on the shoulder. "Is the exchange student bringing pajamas?"

Reese and I looked at Dewey. "Yes," I said. Then I turned back to Reese. "You can't make him your slave, you can't beat him up, and you can't make us look bad in front of my class."

Reese burst out laughing. "Like I care what the Krelboynes think of us? This kid is so mine!"

"Reese!" I yelled, giving him a shove. The next thing I knew we were rolling around on the floor and hitting each other. I'm not sure how. Sometimes that happens with me and Reese.

Dewey scooted over on the couch and changed the channel. No one heard the doorbell ring.

"Is somebody going to get that?" Mom yelled, coming down the hall. She was dressed in shorts and a T-shirt and carrying an armful of sheets to put on the bed for the exchange student. She stepped over me and Reese as we rolled past her into the hall and jerked open the front door. "Yes?" she demanded when the door was open.

My teacher gave her a big smile. "Hi!" she exclaimed, peering past Mom into the house.

Mom smiled back. "Hal!" she called. "The exchange student is here. Come in here!"

Reese and I immediately stopped fighting and looked up.

"I thought he wasn't going to be here until this afternoon!" I said. Nothing was going as planned.

Reese grinned and jumped up. He cracked his knuckles slowly, preparing to show the new kid who was boss. I ran after him to the door as Dewey wrapped himself around Mom. Dad came in from the kitchen.

The teacher smiled nervously at my family: Mom, Dad, and three boys in their underwear. She looked like she was having serious second thoughts about leaving a kid here.

"So?" said Mom. "Where is he?"

"He?" said the teacher. "Oh, you mean your student. Right here." The teacher stepped aside and we saw . . .

"That's a girl," said Reese, as if we couldn't see that.

Mom broke into a big smile. "A girl!" she cried. "Well, come on in!"

Mom reached out and drew the girl into the house. We crowded around her, staring. We couldn't help it.

"This is Camellia," the teacher said, handing Dad a couple of suitcases. We were speechless, which doesn't happen often. "She's from Oakdale. Her father will come to pick her up next Sunday."

"He's working a double shift today," Camellia said. "May is the number one month for disposable pen sales."

I looked at Camellia and she looked back. She was about my height with long dark braids and gold-framed glasses. Behind the glasses her pale gray eyes were magnified and seemed to float at me out of her face. I felt like she was sizing me up. I knew I was sizing her up. I realized I was in my underwear but there was really nothing I could do about that.

"Hi," Camellia said.

"Hi," I said. Dad put Camellia's luggage down on the floor. There was a suitcase, a knapsack and a strangely shaped case with a handle. Dewey stepped behind Mom.

"Welcome to our family," Mom said. "This is Reese, and Malcolm. This is Dewey." She stepped aside to introduce Dewey but he ducked behind her again.

"Pleased to meet you," Camellia said. She had a lot of freckles.

"So where's the exchange student?" said Reese.

I stared at him. "Reese, she's right there."

"But that's a girl," he said. He was really having trouble taking this in.

"There is no boy," I said. "She's it."

"Did you think it was a boy?" The teacher asked. "I guess I should have said something. I didn't think it would be a problem. . . ."

"Problem?" Mom said. "Are you kidding? This is great! Hal, look, it's a girl!"

Dad smiled. "A girl," he said. "What do you know. That's something."

"Let's get you settled," said Mom, putting her arm around Camellia. "Camellia, I love that name!"

The teacher started to follow. "I have some suggested activities that you can all do together," she said, clutching a bunch of papers stapled together. I could see there were a lot of charts and diagrams. Nothing that anyone would really want to do.

Mom glanced at the papers and hustled the teacher out the door. "We'll give you a call if we run out of ideas," she said, shutting the door before turning back to Camellia. I watched Mom and Dad take Camellia down the hall. There was a little squeak behind me as the letter slot in the door opened and the teacher shoved the suggested activity pack into the house where it fell on the rug.

"This is not turning out the way I expected," I noted.

"Is she going to sleep in my bed?" asked Dewey.

Mom suddenly stopped and whirled around. "Oh my gosh," she said. "Hal, where's she going to sleep? When we assumed our guest would be a boy, I made a bed in the boys' room, but she's not, so she can't sleep there."

"She *can't* sleep there," I repeated emphatically. Dad held out his hands helplessly. I was kind of hoping Camellia would realize there was no place for her and go home, but she didn't.

"Wait a minute," Mom said. "What am I thinking?

We have a perfectly good room for Camellia. *She* can just go ahead and take the boys' room!"

I gasped. Dewey's mouth dropped open. Reese just stood there in shock.

"Mom," I said. "Where are *we* going to sleep?"

Mom waved her hand dismissively. "The sofa in the living room — so you'll have to squoosh a little. Think of it as brotherly bonding."

This girl hasn't been here for five minutes, and already she's booted us from our room? "What happens if Francis comes home?" Okay, I knew that was a stupid thing to say, since Francis won't be home this week, but I couldn't think of anything else.

"Who's Francis?" Camellia asked me. She focused her floating gray eyes on me. Before I knew it, I was answering her. I couldn't help it. How did she make me do that?

"Francis is my brother," I said. "He's at Marlin Academy. It's a military school. But he's coming home . . . " I paused. "This summer," I added.

"Hal, bring Camellia's bags into the boys' room!" called Mom.

Camellia followed, leaving the three of us in the hallway.

"No way she's booting us," said Reese. "That's so wrong."

"I know," I said. "Francis's corner of the room is, like, sacred."

There aren't that many things that me and my

brothers agree on? But one of them is Francis. He's the coolest and nobody goes in his part of the room, even when he isn't there.

Before we could think of what to do the phone rang and I picked it up. "Hello?" I said. "Francis!"

Francis was calling from the pay phone at his school. He was whispering, so I could tell he didn't want anyone else in the rec room at school to overhear what he was telling me. "Malcolm, I need you to do something for me."

Reese and Dewey crowded close to me to hear Francis's voice. "Francis," I said. "We have a major situation here. There's this girl staying with us for a week? Mom's booting us and putting her in our room."

"We tried to stop her," Reese put in. "We swear."

Francis cut him off impatiently. "Listen, I've got bigger problems," he said. "I'm sending Mom a gift for Mother's Day. It's in a package addressed to her, but I want you to intercept it."

"Why?" I asked.

"I had to slip something else into the package. You have to take it out and get rid of it before Mom opens her present."

"Sure," I said. "What is it?"

"It's a nose," said Francis.

Reese and I exchanged confused looks.

"I chiseled it off the statue by the front gates of General Marlin in protest of the school's new laundry policy. People are taking it a lot harder than I thought. If Mom finds out I did it I can forget about coming home for the summer."

"No way, man," said Reese. "You have to come home."

"Don't worry about your nose, Francis," I vowed. "We'll take care of everything."

CHAPTER THREE

"Boys," Mom called. "Dinner's ready!"

When I walked into the kitchen the table was all set and the napkins were folded to look like animals.

"What are those?" Reese asked, picking one up and examining it.

"It looks like a swan," Dad offered.

"Aren't those cute?" Mom said, carrying a plate of fried chicken to the table. "Camellia offered to help me set the table. She knows how to make origami napkin animals!"

Reese and I tried not to laugh as Dewey and Dad decided which animals they wanted for their napkins. Dad chose a flamingo and Dewey took the monkey, named it Jo-Jo, and refused to unfold it ever.

"Camellia, you sit next to Malcolm," Mom said. "Malcolm, Camellia has an IQ of 166. That's just one point higher than yours."

That bothered me, but what was I going to say about it? I unfolded my walrus and put it on my lap.

"I saw a bowl in the living room," Camellia said. "The one with the pink-and-purple butterfly painted on it? Did you make that, Lois?"

Reese, Dewey and I all looked up at once. Did this girl just call my mother Lois?

Mom's face turned red. "Oh, that old thing?" she said. "I made that years ago in a pottery class."

"She was pretty good," Dad said, giving Mom a wink. "She made a pencil holder shaped like a guitar that was far out. It's in my office."

I looked from my mom to my dad. How come I didn't know this stuff? I'd looked at that butterfly bowl a million times and didn't know my mom made it. I always thought they found it at a tag sale or something.

"So Camellia," Mom said. "What do you do in your genius class?"

I opened my mouth to answer and then I realized Mom wasn't talking to me. I hate it when she asks me that question every day. But now she was asking Camellia and I didn't like that, either.

Camellia sat up a little straighter. "Yesterday, we created a medieval city. I was the bishop!"

"I was his lordship's rat catcher," I muttered. How come when my class played medieval city I got the worst job? "I got the plague and died."

Everyone looked at me strangely. There's a reason I never talk about my Krelboyne experiences at home. I felt my face getting red. Reese snorted. Dewey and Jo-Jo giggled.

"You look okay now," Dad said.

I frowned down at my plate. "I'm fine. Forget it."

Camellia wiped the corners of her mouth with her napkin. "After school, I take clog dancing," she said.

"Clog dancing!" Mom said. "Hal, did you hear that?"

Dad looked up from his peas. "I like dancing, don't I?"

"You sure do," Mom said. "We saw *Flashdance* five times."

"You're kidding," I said. This was getting ridiculous. "Do you realize that's four hundred and eighty minutes of your life you'll never get back?"

"Malcolm!" Mom said in a tone of voice that meant I was dangerously close to being in trouble if I said anything else like that.

What was going on here? I was getting yelled at and everything was going the way Camellia wanted. This wasn't how dinner was supposed to go in my house.

My mom turned to Camellia again. "What else do you like to do, Camellia?"

Camellia beamed. "I also play the French horn."

"Jo-Jo plays the French horn," said Dewey.

"He does not," I muttered before Reese had a chance.

"Your mother plays the French horn," Dad said.

"What?" I said. I wasn't sure how many more big surprises about my parents I could stand.

"I haven't played in years," said Mom. "Not since high school, when I was first chair in the stage band. But I couldn't play now."

"Sure you could," Camellia said. "Once you're one with the horn, you never forget. I brought mine. It's in my room."

"Our room," I corrected her under my breath.

"Mine's in the attic," Mom said. "I know just where it is. It's next to the boys' old potties!"

A piece of chicken fell out of Reese's open mouth. "Tell me she didn't just say *potties*," he said. Mom didn't seem to notice. She was too busy running upstairs with Camellia to get her french horn out of the attic.

Reese watched them go, shaking his head. "What's going on?" he asked me.

"I don't know," I said. "But it has to stop."

"What's clog dancing anyway?" asked Reese.

"Dad, you have to do something," I said.

"About what?" asked Dad, who had been making designs on his plate with his peas and mashed potatoes.

I sighed. "About Camellia!"

"She seems like a nice girl," said Dad pleasantly.

"I just think she's weird," I said. "Even her name is weird. Camellia? What kind of name is that?"

Dad chuckled.

Reese, Dewey and I exchanged frightened looks, like we always did when Dad chuckled like that.

"You want to hear something funny?" Dad said. "When we were picking names for all of you, every time we picked a girl's name Mom chose Camellia."

"What?" I said.

"Think about it," said Dad. "Each and every one of you might have been Camellia."

Dad smiled around the table at us. We all looked at each other in horror, each of us imagining himself being saddled with the name Camellia.

Dewey clutched his napkin monkey to his chest and shivered. "Are we going to turn into girls?"

I thought this exchange student was going to be trouble. As it turns out, she's worse than trouble. First of all, she's a girl. I like girls. I mean, they're okay. But not in my house, staying in my room, pulling the strings in my family, and filling the house with napkin animals. If I wanted to wipe my mouth with a walrus, I'd go to the North Pole. The good news is, me and Reese are getting out of the house this afternoon with Mom. The bad news is, we're getting our hair cut. I know that doesn't sound like much, but believe me, for us, it's very bad news.

CHAPTER FOUR

"**M**alcolm! Reese! Hurry up!" Mom called. It was Sunday. Time for our appointment with the barber. I pulled a pair of socks out of my drawer and put them on. Reese stood in front of the mirror, fixing his hair.

"Why do you care what your hair looks like?" I asked him. "You're getting it cut anyway."

Reese gave me that look, like I'd just asked a really stupid question. "Because the barbershop is in the mall," he said. "Girls are in the mall. Wendy Finnerman might be at the mall. Any questions?"

My brother Reese can be really weird. I mean, here he is spending an hour fixing his hair in case he sees this girl he likes. If we run into her, he'll shoot a straw wrapper into her face or something and laugh at her. It's his way. I don't question it.

"Boys!" Mom called again. "If you're not out here by the time I count to ten I'm telling the barber to make you both look like your class pictures from first grade!"

Those photos were hanging up in the hallway. I look like a Keebler elf gone bad, and Reese looks like son of Moe. You know, from the Three Stooges? Me and Reese ran downstairs.

Mom was waiting and beside her was — Camellia. She was wearing a jacket, like she was planning to go somewhere.

"It's about time," Mom said when we got to the door. "Camellia's been ready for fifteen minutes."

Reese and I looked Camellia up and down. "Ready for what?" Reese asked.

"Camellia's coming with us," Mom said, smiling.

Camellia tried to smile, but it kind of faded when she met Reese's unfriendly eye. "I'm doing a study on how much money is in the average mall fountain," she said, like anybody *normal* would do that. Wait. *I* do that.

Sixty-three dollars and eighteen cents. That's the average amount of change in our fountain at our mall. I'd done the math, but I wasn't going to tell her that. I didn't believe that was why she wanted to go to the mall anyway. She was up to something.

"Mom," I said. "Seriously, can't you think of any better way to entertain our genius guest?" I grabbed the teacher's instruction pack from the table where it had gotten tossed. "There's got to be something in here that's more challenging than dragging Camellia around the mall with us and making her count change in the fountain." *Challenging* was a word they always used to describe the kind of things genius kids should be doing, so I knew my mom would pay attention.

I watched Mom carefully. Her eyebrow twitched, she looked up to the right, and she chewed the inside of her cheek — that meant she was actually thinking about what I said.

"You may be right," she said, looking apologetically at Camellia. "I don't want to bore you."

Camellia was watching me. Her gray eyes seemed to float out toward me and then pull back. "I'll stay here," she said. But what I heard was, "This means war."

I had just foiled her plans and gotten her stuck in the house with Dewey all day. I dropped the activity pack back on the table. Mom dug her car keys out of her purse and turned to Camellia.

"You and I will go shopping next week," she promised her. "Just a girls' day out."

Camellia smiled, but she stopped smiling when I went past her.

Sunday at the mall was pretty crowded, so we had to drive around the parking lot a few times. Finally we saw a lady coming out to her car. Mom sat and waited for her to pull out of her space. She was taking a long time, so Mom glared at her until she peeled out of the space with a screech of her tires. It never failed. Even complete strangers were cowed into submission by Mom's Road Rage Look.

As we walked through the mall, it seemed like

every store was selling something either me or Reese really wanted, and it was on sale. "Mom, I need these sneakers," Reese explained in front of the sporting goods store. "My old ones are worn down. I've got no support. It's throwing off my layup."

"Reese," Mom said. "Your old ones are only two months old. They're practically new."

"Malcolm can wear them," Reese offered.

"No, he can't," I said loudly. Sticking your foot in one of Reese's shoes was like sticking it into a big, wet mouth. "Hey, Mom," I said. "Can I get the new Nightwing comic? I heard Two-Face has escaped from the mental asylum and he's threatening to blow up the city!"

"I don't know why you read those things," Mom said. "But you can buy them with your own money."

My mom doesn't understand the glory that is the comic book form. As we passed a jewelry store, Mom stopped and looked in the window. There was nothing in there but a bunch of earrings and things.

Reese walked ahead. "Mom," he called. "They're giving away free transmission checkups! Can we get one?"

Mom turned away from the jewelry store window with a sigh. "No," she said. "But you can get a haircut."

Mom marched us to the barbershop without letting us stop or look to the left or right at the stores. Finally we were both seated in barber chairs next to each other with those weird smocks wrapped around us.

"Can you shave something into the back of my head?" Reese asked the barber as he came over with his electric razor. "I want it to say 750,056,943. It's my high score on Mortal Kombat."

"You wish," I said.

Reese jerked his head around. The barber jumped away with the razor. "It is too," he said. "Ask anyone who was there. I got up to level five and I would've gone farther but somebody bumped my elbow."

"And then you woke up," I said, jerking my own head away from my barber's scissors. He placed his hands on the sides of my head and turned me back to the mirror.

"Can you do something about this?" Mom asked the guy cutting my hair. She grabbed a hunk of my hair from the back of my head and pulled on it hard so my chin jerked up. "See, right here. There's a piece that sticks straight up no matter what he does."

"Yeah," yelled Reese. "He looks like an alien and it's pretty embarrassing for the rest of the family."

"Shut up, Reese," I yelled back, spinning my chair around. I think I hit something with it. I think it was the barber, because he dropped the scissors.

"Boys!" Mom said sharply. "Sit still or the barber's going to slice an ear off and it'll be your own fault. And I'm not packing it in ice to take it to the hospital."

"But, Mom," I protested, spinning back around. The barber was getting out his electric razor to do the back of my neck.

"But nothing," said Mom.

For a second I said nothing. But only for a second. Then I turned to Reese and said, "I'd rather look like an alien than a monkey that's been strategically shaved to resemble a person."

Reese started to respond, but then he hesitated.

"Strategically what?" he asked.

"I just called you a monkey," I clarified. The trouble with fighting with Reese was that whenever I get in a really good shot, he misses it and I have to explain it. Now that he got it, he was ready to hit back.

Reese spun in his chair and tried to kick me, but I spun in the other direction and grabbed a can of something called mousse that looked a lot like whipped cream when I squirted it at Reese.

Reese jumped out of his chair and jumped on me. He stood on the footrest of my chair so he could hit me from above. I blocked him with one arm and hit at his stomach with the other. As we fought, the chair spun slowly around like a music box. Only more violent.

"Malcolm! Reese!" Mom screeched, pulling Reese off me and placing him back in his own chair. "I have had enough of this!" She glared at both of us, one after the other. She picked up an electric razor and buzzed it menacingly at each of us. "If either one of you moves once more, I am personally going to give you your first shaving lesson. And it's not going to be on your face."

Reese and I both turned back to the mirror, watching each other out of the corners of our eyes. Round one was over, but I could tell the fight had just begun. We might not get out of this barbershop alive.

CHAPTER FIVE

"**W**ell, that's one more barber we can't go to any-more," Mom announced as she pushed me and Reese through the front door. Reese had a large Band-Aid on his forehead from when I kicked his chair as the barber was leaning over with the razor. My ear hadn't been sliced off like Mom said, just nicked pretty badly at the top. You'd be surprised at how much an ear can bleed.

Mom grabbed Reese as he was heading for the TV. "Don't even think about it, mister," she said. "That TV does not get turned on. The two of you are going to sit staring at a blank screen until dinner and you are going to think about all those kids who have no hair at all. You kids don't know how lucky you are."

Of course we did. Mom told us all the time how lucky we were.

Reese flopped onto his side of the sofa bed. I sat on my side. For a second we were quiet and then we both started laughing. We couldn't help it. We ruled that barbershop.

"So how long do you think it will be before that glob of dippity-do falls off the ceiling?" I asked.

"I don't know," said Reese. "But there had better be

someone underneath it when it does or I'm going to be bummed."

We both imagined the look on the person's face when this happened. It's too bad we couldn't be there to see it, but we were banned from ever going back there.

"I guess we'd better get Mom a killer Mother's Day present after today," I said. "But it was worth it."

"I already got one," said Reese. "I traded my extra copy of Double Dragon to this guy in my class for a state-of-the-art exercise ball."

I stared at him. "An exercise ball?" I said. "You mean one of those big rubber balls like they used to have in Dewey's preschool for the kids to bounce on? What's Mom going to do with that?"

Reese rolled his eyes like he was going to have to educate me again. "Dude, this is scientifically designed exercise equipment. It's the official exercise ball of the WWF Smackdown Challenge."

"So in other words," I said. "It's totally not for Mom and you'll be the only one who uses it."

We heard running footsteps in the hall. Dewey rushed in, and crawled under the couch. We let him stay there for a few minutes. Dewey got chased under the couch, table, or bed by imaginary monsters about twice a week on average. But he was usually out within thirty seconds. This was some monster.

"Come out, Dewey," I said with a sigh. Sometimes we had to help him or else he wouldn't come out, even to go to the bathroom.

"No!" Dewey's voice said from under the couch.

Reese rolled his eyes. "Dewey, don't be a total dip-wad. It degrades both you and us."

I got down onto the floor so I could look Dewey in the eye. He was curled up in a ball, clutching his head in his hands. "Dewey," I said. "We made the bad monster go away. He'll be gone for at least two hours. It's totally safe. For now."

Dewey just shook his head and shut his eyes tight. Something weird was going on. I motioned to Reese, and he got down on the floor with me. We each grabbed one of Dewey's feet and together we dragged him out from under the couch.

"No! No!" Dewey cried, trying to hold on to the threads in the rug. "She's going to get me!"

Reese and I looked at each other. She? It was em-barrassing enough that Dewey was always being chased by imaginary monsters. If he was going to start being chased by female imaginary mon-sters . . . that was just too much.

We sat him up and pinned him against the couch. Reese pulled the lamp down from the end table and twisted it so the bulb shined right into Dewey's face. Dewey squirmed and tried to keep his eyes shut, but I held his head. I have no idea if this light-in-the-face thing really works. But they always do it in cartoons when they want to make someone talk. It's pretty fun.

"Dewey, this is a three-way lightbulb," Reese said menacingly. He clicked it quickly through all three levels of brightness, then put it back on the lowest level. "We've got all day. We're going to break you."

That was my cue to play the good brother. "Dewey," I said. "Whatever it is, you can tell us. We just want to help you." Reese and I both smiled.

Dewey kicked and tried to escape, but it was hopeless. Finally, he started to talk. "I promised her I wouldn't tell," he said. "If I do she'll send her killer robot to get me!"

"Told on who?" I asked. "Who's got a killer robot?" If somebody in this house had a killer robot, I wanted to know about it.

"Camellia!" Dewey whispered. "She made me tell her things. She and her robot."

Reese frowned at me. "That exchange student?"

This was getting weird. "Dewey, what are you talking about?" I said.

Dewey took a couple of deep breaths. "I said I was going to tell on her. She said if I did her robot would come to me at night and zap me with its laser eyes. Then it would twist my arms off and put me in the dishwasher."

Okay, it didn't take much for us to scare Dewey but we'd known him for life. I'd never seen anyone else find his panic buttons so fast.

Reese stuck his face right up to Dewey's. "Dewey, that's totally stupid. You don't even fit in the dishwasher, remember?"

That's when it hit me. Camellia might not have a killer robot like Dewey thought, but she had done something that Dewey could tell on her for. If Mom found out about it, Camellia could forget about taking over this family.

"Dewey," I said. "What did Camellia do that she doesn't want you to tell?"

Dewey shut his mouth and shook his head. Then he put his hands over his mouth. No matter how much Reese and I poked, shook, and threatened him, he wouldn't talk.

"I don't get it," said Reese. He looked a little worried. "How can he be more afraid of some girl than he is of me?" He cracked his knuckles for reassurance.

"Not only that," I said. "How could Camellia get Dewey so scared he won't tell on her? We've been trying to keep him from telling on us since he learned to talk."

"It's weird," Reese said. "I always thought that if somebody figured out how to do it, it would be you. Camellia beat you to it."

"That's it," I said. "This ends now."

The two of us picked Dewey up so we were each holding one of his elbows and his feet dangled off the ground. We marched up to Camellia's — I mean, our — door and knocked.

Camellia opened the door like she was expecting us.

"I didn't tell!" Dewey cried. "They tried to make me, but I wouldn't!"

"You're a good boy, Dewey," Camellia said. Then she turned to me and Reese. "Can I help you?"

"What did you do to my brother?" I demanded.

"I didn't do anything," Camellia said. "I told him I wouldn't, as long as he kept his promise." She pushed her glasses up on her face so her eyes got even bigger.

Reese went into warrior mode. "We're going to find out what you did," he promised. "And when we do . . ."

His threat was cut off by Camellia's matter-of-fact response. "I'll tell you what I did," she said, putting her hands on her hips. "I already told Lois. Dewey saw me trying on some of her makeup. I should have asked first, but I knew she wouldn't mind and I had nothing else to do because everyone else was at the mall. Lois and I are going to get makeovers next week."

I could feel Dewey relax in my grip so his feet sank down to the floor again.

I tried to figure this out. Camellia took Mom's makeup, and for punishment Mom was buying her more makeup. How did she make that work? When me and Reese used Mom's makeup to paint our bodies like they did in *Braveheart* she made us stand in the driveway in our underwear while she hosed it off.

"That is totally unfair," said Reese. "You should have to stand in the corner for five hours or spin until you throw up or . . . something."

This was unbelievable. Camellia had totally dodged my "I know what you did" attack by telling

Mom herself, and she had gotten herself out of trouble better than I ever had in my life. She had the run of the house and I was supposed to be quarantined in the TV room with the TV off with Reese all afternoon appreciating my hair.

"Should you guys really be here?" Camellia said. "I think Lois wanted you to stay in the living room and think about your behavior at the barber's. I wouldn't want you to get in trouble again."

She smiled and shut the door in our faces.

"Who's Lois?" Dewey asked.

Reese glared at him. "Shut up, buttmunch," he said.

Then he glared at me. "This is all your fault," he said. "She's your exchange student."

"What's an exchange student?" Dewey asked.

"It's a kid that gets exchanged for another kid," I said impatiently. "She comes here and another kid goes to her house."

Dewey thought for a second. "Who's going to live at her house?" he asked.

Reese and I didn't hesitate before we answered Dewey.

"You," we both said at the same time.

CHAPTER SIX

The next morning was the first morning ever that I actually wished I was walking to school with Dewey. Since Camellia was in my class, I had to walk with her while Dewey hid behind Reese.

"So Malcolm," Camellia said. "Do you take turns walking Dewey to school?"

"Why?" I said. "Is your killer robot available to do it?"

Camellia laughed. "Your brother's a little jumpy, isn't he?" she said. "You've trained him well. Thanks to you and Reese he already thinks there's a monster in the dishwasher and that your dad's a werewolf. It was one short step to killer robot."

I had to smile. It was almost a year since we told Dewey about Dad being a werewolf and he was still hiding from him when there was a full moon. But how did Camellia know that? Dewey must have really spilled his guts. There was no telling what she knew. It was like having a spy living in your house.

"That was different," I said. "He's our brother. You're nobody."

Wait. That's not what I meant.

"I mean, you don't understand because you're not part of our family . . . " Camellia was giving me that look again. The one with the floaty eyes. "I mean you're not . . . "

"Forget it," Camellia said coldly. "Believe me, I thank the goddess every day that I'm not."

Then she marched off ahead of me into the trailer with her long braids swinging behind her like two angry snakes. It was hard for me to make myself follow her in. But at least in class things would be back to normal. She couldn't take my place there.

I opened the door and climbed into the trailer. Camellia was standing at the blackboard, holding the chalk, with a big smile on her face, and everyone was applauding. I couldn't believe what I saw. In the five seconds since she'd gone through the door Camellia had solved my math problem. Nobody even noticed I came in. Even Stevie had rolled his wheelchair to her side and was acting like *she* was his best friend, instead of me.

I went to my seat and took out my books by myself. Luckily the teacher came in and brought Camellia to the front of the room. Stevie wheeled himself over to me.

"When . . . did . . . you . . . get . . . here?" he asked me.

"I came in right after Camellia — only nobody noticed. You won't believe what this weekend was like," I began.

"She's . . . great," Stevie said, looking at Camellia. Unbelievable.

"Okay, class," the teacher said. "I think you've all met Camellia, who spent the weekend at Malcolm's house and she's just fine!" The teacher sounded unmistakably relieved by that. "Camellia has agreed to tell us all a little bit about what that was like for her. Camellia?"

I nudged Stevie. "What is this, *National Geographic*? Camellia's going to talk about her life at my house like we're a tribe of pygmies? What's there to talk about? We're just a regular family."

That was a lie. We're not a regular family. Now the whole class was going to know just how weird my family is.

Camellia took her place at the front of the class and flipped her braids. "Well," she began, like she was really going to enjoy this. "Malcolm's family is really great. First of all, his mom is really cool. When she talks, people listen. His dad is really funny and he loves Malcolm's mom a lot."

This made half the class — the girl half — sigh and look at me in a way that made me seriously uncomfortable. What was Camellia talking about anyway? Where was she getting this stuff?

"Malcolm has three brothers," Camellia went on. "The oldest one, Francis, is away at school and everyone really misses him, especially Malcolm."

Okay, how did she know *that*? I did not tell her anything like that.

"His next brother is Reese. Reese is a `thought-as-action' kind of creature. If he uses his powers for good, he can be a positive force in the world. Left unchecked he could run amok and destroy whole villages."

I felt my mouth drop open. I've known Reese all my life and I couldn't have explained him any better. I looked around and saw the rest of the class with their heads bent down, scribbling notes on my family. Even the teacher was taking notes.

"And then there's Dewey," said Camellia with a little smile. "Dewey is the youngest but should not be underestimated. He's a keen observer, and life in Malcolm's family has taught him to use others' strengths against them in combat."

Wow, I thought. She's good. Even I was fascinated, waiting for what she was going to say next about my own family.

"And in the middle of it all," Camellia said, "there's young master Malcolm."

I jumped in my chair. Nobody calls me "young master Malcolm," except my brother Francis, and Camellia didn't even *know* Francis. Having someone call me that in class made me feel like I was having one of those dreams where I accidentally go to school with no clothes on? Am I the only person who has that dream?

Camellia caught my eye and paused before she went on.

"Malcolm loves his family," she said. "But he's secretly afraid of being replaced. Sometimes it disturbs his sleep so that he tosses and turns and calls out people's names. By the way, which one of you is Julie?"

Every single head in the class swiveled to look at me. I knew they were all thinking the same thing: Julie Houlerman, a girl in my old class.

Eraserhead looked at me like I was some new kind of bug he'd never seen. Three girls in the corner giggled. And Stevie grinned at me. "Why . . . young . . . master . . . Malcolm."

Once when I was little, my brother Francis accidentally dropped me into a freezing lake. It felt a little like that now, only about ten times worse.

Where was Camellia getting this stuff? Julie Houlerman is my friend. But I do not dream about her. At least, I didn't think I did until this moment. And how would Camellia know what I said in my sleep. . . ?

Unless Dewey told her.

I waited until after school to talk to the teacher. We'd had Camellia for a whole weekend. It was somebody else's turn now.

"Sit down, Malcolm," the teacher said with a smile. She was the only person who could get Camellia out of my house. "Talk to me," the teacher said.

"It's about Camellia," I began.

"I'm so glad you're getting along," said the teacher. "I have to admit I was a little worried about leaving her with your family."

The teacher made a speech about coping skills, family dynamics, and reckless endangerment that I couldn't understand at all. When she was finished I said, "Isn't there somebody else who can take her?"

The teacher blinked like this bird that smacked into our window once and knocked itself senseless. "But she really likes your family."

"I know," I said. "That's the problem. She likes my family too much. It's just . . . look, she's a really nice girl, but it's weird having her in my house."

The teacher's face got all soft. Her eyes crinkled up and a big smile spread over her face. "Oh Malcolm," she singsonged. "Now I see what the real problem is. You have a little crush on Camellia, don't you?"

"What? No! What are you talking about?"

"Malcolm, you don't have to pretend with me. I'm your teacher and your friend. It's only natural that you would like a girl that you have so much in common with."

I didn't know which was worse: the teacher thinking I had a crush on Camellia or thinking me and Camellia had a lot in common.

"Look, forget I said anything," I said quickly, picking up my knapsack and heading for the door.

"If you want to talk about your feelings some more, Malcolm, you can always call me," the teacher called after me.

I slammed the trailer door behind me. It looked like I was stuck with Camellia for the rest of the week.

Honestly, how much worse could this week get? It felt like I couldn't make anything work anymore. Everything I tried to do, Camellia got there first and I knew she was doing it on purpose. I know that because if I was doing what she was doing, I would be doing it on purpose. First she terrorized Dewey in a way that even Reese was impressed by. Then she humiliated me in class beyond anything I'd ever dreamed could happen. And I've had some pretty humiliating dreams. I can't even go home to get away from her because she's there, waiting, in my room. She's probably plotting her next move right now.

CHAPTER SEVEN

I opened the front door to my house and looked around. Luckily, Camellia was nowhere to be seen. But Reese was there. He grabbed me by the collar as soon as I walked in and slammed me against the wall. But I could tell from his eyes he wasn't angry. He just wanted to talk to me.

"What's the matter?" I said. I was sure Camellia had done something else.

"Nothing," said Reese, grinning proudly. "It's all taken care of."

"What's taken care of?"

"Francis's problem, you dork," said Reese. "It's history. The package came this afternoon. Mom never even saw it. I put it somewhere safe. Somewhere nobody will find it."

That was a relief. At least there was one less problem in my life. The idea of Francis not coming home this summer was worse than anything Camellia could dish up. Now that I knew Francis would be home soon, everything seemed a whole lot easier. Even my total humiliation in class was something I could get over. Right? I hoped so, anyway. If Camellia was going to stay with us for a whole week, I would just go and tell her she'd better not pull anything like that again.

I walked down the hall, to my room. In a couple more days, she'd be gone and things would be back to normal. I actually envisioned my room — with me back in it. It made me feel better already. My posters, which cover the hole where Francis's lava lamp exploded because he'd left it on the radiator. Reese's amazing CD collection and a machine to dub them. Francis's videos that said they were one thing on the box but were really something else. He had a big gorilla that he had won at an amusement park. He dressed it up in different outfits, like right now? It was dressed in a Hawaiian shirt and a baseball cap, holding a soda can.

Then after all that visualizing, I couldn't help myself.

I knocked on my door.

"Come in," Camellia called from inside.

I opened the door. "Look, Camellia, I really need to talk to . . . "

The words died in my throat. The first thing that hit me was the smell. It was sickly sweet, like a sugar cookie. I think it was vanilla and it was coming from a big, fat candle burning on the desk. Then there were the rainbows. They were everywhere: on the walls, on the floor, on the ceiling. Camellia had hung these suncatchers in all the windows that split the light into the spectrum of colors. There was music playing but it certainly didn't come from Reese's collection. It was some woman singing with a guitar that wasn't even electric.

Then I saw the gorilla. He was draped in a big pink scarf and holding a bouquet of flowers. This wasn't my room — this was Girl City!

At the desk sat Camellia. She was hunched over with a tool kit and parts from about four different dolls. She'd built a super doll with wires coming out of its head that were attached to a battery pack. Camellia flipped the switch and the doll rose up off the desk like Frankenbarbie and walked toward me. Its eyes flashed red laser beams. I owed Dewey an apology. She did have a killer robot. It was so cool. I wish I'd made it. Wait a minute? What was I saying? I bolted back to the living room before I started asking her what voltage she used.

At dinner Dewey still made a place for Jo-Jo beside his plate. The napkin monkey was covered in stains from different meals. Dad had begun talking to Jo-Jo, too, because he was such a good listener. Reese was still grinning and congratulating himself on the way he handled his mission for Francis. The nose was hidden safely somewhere in the house. After dinner I would have to get him to show me where it was. Then I could take the incriminating nose out of the package and bury it.

In the middle of it all was Camellia. She got Mom

and Dad talking about more things she liked and nobody else cared about, like how inchworms raise their young in the wild.

"That reminds me," Mom said. "I got a call from Francis's school today." From the sound of her voice I could tell she wasn't happy about it. "Do you know what some little creep did? Somebody chiseled off the nose of that beautiful statue of General Marlin. Do you know how hard that's going to be to replace? I hope they catch whoever did it and lock him up in solitary until next spring!"

Reese and I tried really hard not to look at each other while Mom was talking about the nose.

Reese laughed unconvincingly. "That nose is probably a thousand miles away by now. The guy probably mailed it to Siberia."

That made Camellia look up. "Wait a minute," she said, getting the attention back on herself. "I think I have something for you, Lois."

Camellia left the table and ran down the hall. She returned a second later with a brown paper package. I stared at it, then I looked at Reese. The look on his face told me everything.

"I found this in my room this afternoon, behind the gorilla," Camellia said, handing Mom a package addressed to her from Francis's school. "It's addressed to you. I thought maybe you left it there by accident."

Mom frowned at the package. Of course, she'd never seen it before. She opened it. First she saw a

50

wrapped Mother's Day present. "How sweet!" she said. Then she saw a piece of granite. She turned it over in her hands until she saw nostrils.

Her eyes bugged out, she sucked in her breath, and then she started yelling. "Which one of you hid this for him?" she demanded. Her gaze moved from one face to the next at the table and quickly zeroed in on me and Reese.

"You are in so much trouble," Mom promised. "But not as much trouble as your brother — FRANCIS!"

Mom got up from the table with a bang and went straight for the phone. Reese looked at me with panic in his eyes. Dewey tried to comfort Jo-Jo.

Good job, Camellia, I thought. You just destroyed our perfect family dinner even better than I could. Wait! Now she's better than me at that, too!

Dad looked at Reese and shook his head sadly. "You should have let Malcolm hide it," he said.

At the phone, Mom was talking to Francis's school. "You tell him to call his mother," she said. "As soon as he gets back from choir practice!"

Mom slammed down the phone and came back to the table. "Statue disfigurement!" she said. "That's all I need. And you're just as guilty as he is."

"I didn't do it," Reese said. He always panicked when Mom got like this.

"We were just keeping the package until Mother's Day," I said. "I swear! We didn't know there was any nose in it."

Mom grabbed my chin and looked into my eyes. I

tried to fight it, but she was too strong for me. "He didn't mean it!" I yelled. "He was just protesting the school's laundry policy!"

Mom turned to Reese and fixed her gaze on him. "It seemed like a good idea at the time!" Reese yelled.

"That's no excuse for cutting off a nose," Mom said.

"How does he sneeze?" Dewey asked.

"Not very often," said Dad.

"Hal!" Mom yelled. "This is serious. Your son's a vandal!"

The next thing I knew we were all yelling at once. I thought I heard the phone ring, but it didn't seem like a good time to answer it. I don't know what we were yelling about exactly, but finally we all ran out of breath at the same time. I heard the phone being hung up. It was Camellia.

"That was Francis," she said. "He wanted to talk to you but he had to run to marching practice. He said he was sorry."

Mom made the noise she makes when she's completely lost it — so far Francis is the only person who can make her do it. She just left all the dishes on the table and went to her room. Dad followed her, shaking his head.

As soon as we heard their door shut, I screamed at Reese. "You idiot! Why would you hide it in there? Why didn't you just slip it under Mom's pillow?"

Dewey actually did that once, but I expected a little better from Reese. What was he thinking?

Reese whirled around to Camellia. "This is all your

fault!" he yelled. "Mom would have never found out if you hadn't given her that package. The plan was perfect until you ruined it."

"If it was perfect, I couldn't have ruined it," Camellia said, logically.

Reese just looked stunned. Camellia elaborated like she was explaining one of her math problems.

"If I knew what was in the package, I wouldn't have given it to her," she said. "But it had her name on it and it was just sitting in my — I mean, your — room. Why did you leave the nose in the package anyway? Why didn't you destroy the evidence immediately? What were you saving it for? It seems to me, this is all your fault."

She was absolutely right, but that made it all the more dangerous. You never tell Reese when he's really screwed up or he'll kill you. Even now his face was getting red and he was clenching and unclenching his fists, getting ready to pound on someone. But he wasn't moving.

That's when I realized he wasn't going to hit Camellia. He couldn't hit her — she was a girl. Without hitting, Reese was powerless.

I shook a little as the full impact of the situation hit me. My parents don't yell at her, Reese can't hit her, Dewey's afraid to rat her out, and she blocks my every strategic move.

Camellia was invincible!

CHAPTER EIGHT

Mom grounded us for four days. It was going to be three, but Reese tried to bargain her down.

"That's so unfair," said Reese. "When we announced that Dad got fired over the loudspeaker at your job you only grounded us for two days. I think this is a Code One violation and deserves the same sentence."

He crossed his arms over his chest and regarded Mom coolly.

Did he honestly think that was going to work? Reese has never bested Mom in an argument, but he keeps trying.

Mom's eyes bugged out. Too late, Reese realized his mistake.

"And you obviously didn't learn your lesson, mister," she screamed. "No leaving the house after school until Friday. That's four days!"

"Nice going, moron," I muttered, punching him in the side.

Reese just shook his head, still trying to figure out what went wrong.

We got a reprieve on Thursday — well, sort of. My dad agreed to take us to the mall when he got home from work so we could get Mom a present. There's something wrong about that. The only time we're let out of the house it's to buy a present for the person who's keeping us there? It's sick, you know?

"Reese, you have more money than that. I know it," I said. We were in the living room — now, our bedroom — after school, waiting for Dad to get home.

"I'm saving up for infrared goggles," he protested.

"Reese," I said. "We have to get Mom a real present. That means spending all our money. All of us."

I'd decided that Mother's Day was going to put me back on top and Camellia back where she belonged — out of my family. Mother's Day was always about us: the boys. After all, without us, Mom wouldn't be a mother.

Reese and I both turned to Dewey, who was standing very still, hoping we wouldn't notice him. Don't ask me how, but over the years Dewey has amassed a fortune that he keeps under his bed. I think it has something to do with all the time he spends digging behind the cushions of the couch. What he didn't eat, he saved.

"Cough it up, Dewey," Reese said.

Dewey produced a mayonnaise jar full of coins and bills. I pulled out a small wad of money from my pocket. So much for that first edition of *Youngblood #1* at the comic book store.

Dad poked his head in. "Are we going somewhere?" he said.

"The mall," I reminded him. "To get Mom's present."

"Right," said Dad. "Mom and Camellia are in the car."

I stared at him. He had to be kidding.

"Dad, Mom can't come with us, because we're buying her present. And Camellia can't come with us because . . . "

"Because she's the enemy," Reese said in a low, serious voice. He still blamed her for us getting grounded.

Dad didn't seem to notice. "We're just giving them a ride to the mall," he said. "They're having a girls' day out. Your mom's really excited."

None of us said anything. We weren't excited.

We climbed into the van. Mom and Dad were in the front seat. Camellia was behind them, sitting by herself. Me, Reese, and Dewey were squeezed together in the backseat. I was in the middle, with Reese's elbow in my ribs as usual. Dewey was on the other side of me and he was sticky.

"This is going to be so much fun," Mom said, strapping on her seat belt. "I always thought I'd go shopping with my daughter someday. The boys hate shopping."

"Because it stinks," Reese explained under his breath.

"My dad doesn't like to shop either," Camellia said. "He says my mom loved to shop and me and my sisters inherited it from her."

Okay, what did that mean? Her mom's not around, obviously, but where is she?

Camellia turned around and looked at me with her floaty eyes. "We lost her a few years ago."

How'd she know I was thinking that? Can she hear my thoughts? Is she hearing this? Hello? Hello . . . ?

We split up as soon as we got through the doors of the mall. Mom and Camellia went off toward the Buttons 'n' Bows Boutique to buy whatever they sold in there. I pulled Reese away from the store where they had spinning hubcaps in the window. "Come on," I said. "We're going to the jewelry store."

I shoved him ahead of me, then I had to go back for Dad who was watching the same hubcaps spin. You'd think he'd be too old for that kind of thing.

So we're in this jewelry store, but what do we do now? I mean, everything looks the same. You'd think Dad would be some help? But he's not. Like for her engagement ring? Dad gave Mom a ring that was a monkey's head with a diamond chip in its mouth. Sounds pretty cool to me, but Mom said it was the ugliest thing she ever saw.

"Look at this!" Reese said, pointing to one of the cases. It was filled with jeweled letter openers. They did look pretty cool. Like the kind of knives people duel with in old movies.

"Mom needs to protect herself at all times," Reese said.

"Reese, they're letter openers, they're not weapons," I told him. His face fell.

Dewey was standing in front of a glass case full of

watches. His head was moving side to side in time with the ticking.

"It should be something she can wear," I said. But what kind of jewelry did Mom wear? I tried to picture her dressed up to go out to dinner. I remembered her yelling at the three of us with her hair up, in a nice dress. I saw shiny things swinging back and forth as she screamed. They were hanging from her ears.

"Earrings!" I said triumphantly.

We ran over to the earring display. For a second we all stared at the case. We didn't even know where to start to pick one. Until we saw...

"Check it out," Reese whispered.

He didn't even have to point. All our eyes — mine, Reese's, Dewey's, and Dad's — were locked on the same pair. These earrings looked like a pair of really cool jaguars. It was like they hung from your ears by their tails. But they had really sharp claws and you could see all their teeth.

And they were pretty too. Their spots were green? I guess those would be emeralds. And their eyes were red.

"And jaguars are perfect for your mother," said Dad. "Grrrrrrrr."

We all looked at him strangely.

"Whatever," said Reese. "Wrap 'em up."

We were so psyched when we met Mom and Camellia by the Twist and Creme to go home.

Camellia had a bunch of packages, but nothing inside them could match our killer present.

When we got home Mom told us to all wait in the living room because she and Camellia had a surprise.

"Are we getting a puppy?" Dewey asked as we all got settled on the couch.

"Not until we find your hamster," said Dad.

"Are you ready?" Mom called.

"Yes," we groaned. How long was she going to drag this out?

"Okay," Mom said. "Here we come!"

Mom and Camellia walked into the living room. They looked the same. I mean really the same. Their new dresses were the same color red. They both had their hair piled on their head and stuck with chopsticks. They looked like Siamese twins. It was the creepiest thing I'd ever seen. It was like those pod people? You know, in *Invasion of the Body Snatchers*? Don't go to sleep, Mom.

Reese's mouth was hanging open.

I looked to Dad. It was up to him to put a stop to this.

"I can't believe it!" Dad said, jumping out of his chair.

Neither could I.

"You'll have to wear these when we go out to dinner. You look so cute!"

Wait. What? They did not look cute. But Dad was

making them turn around and told Dewey to get the camera. Mom and Dad smiled at each other. Camellia stood tucked in between them, beaming up at them both. It would have been a nice family portrait, except that it was my family and I wasn't in it!

It was *Invasion of the Family Snatchers*.

It was time to call in the big guns. After dinner that night, I called Francis. "I've got to tell you about this girl in the house," I began.

"You mean Camellia?" Francis said. "I just got off the phone with her. She's excellent!"

I felt the Hamburger Helper and the cling peaches in heavy syrup sloshing around in my stomach as it flipped over. She had gotten to Francis.

"What do you mean she's excellent?" I demanded. "She's taken over Mom and Dad. She's removed Reese as a threat. She's scared Dewey so much he's stopped snitching and — oh yeah — she totally humiliated me in front of my whole class! I've never been so embarrassed in my life! I'll never recover!"

Francis laughed. He LAUGHED.

"Malcolm, buddy," he said. "No offense, but sometimes you take things a little too seriously. You're always getting totally humiliated and you're embarrassed every time I talk to you. You've got to learn to chill out."

Was Francis right? I mean, maybe I do take things too seriously.

"Anyway, Malcolm," said Francis. "Who cares that you dream about Julie Houlerman?"

I hung up the phone like it had just become radioactive.

How could Francis take her side against me? I was his brother, not her!

... Wasn't I?

The one person I always thought I could count on was Francis. If he can be turned to the Dark Side, nothing is safe. I guess I just have to accept that my whole family's gone crazy. I mean more crazy than they were before.

I feel like Camellia's managed to take my place in my own family. I was the one who made things happen. I was the one who was supposed to keep us out of trouble. I was the one Francis thought was great. Now Camellia was that person. What did that make me? Am I even in the middle anymore?

CHAPTER NINE

Our grounding was really starting to get to Reese. In gym class he busted three dodge balls and sent one kid to the nurse. And the kid was on his own team. I heard all this from Stevie, who had to go to the nurse himself when he inhaled a dust particle during science.

"Your ... brother's ... whacked ... out," Stevie said. "They ... want ... to ... put ... him ... on ... meds ... before ... he ... breaks ... someone's ... arm."

"He'll be okay once we're not grounded anymore," I said. "And as soon as that girl gets out of our house."

"You ... have ... issues ... with ... Camellia ... don't ... you?" said Stevie.

"I don't have issues with her," I said. "I just don't like girls who abduct my parents and replace them with pod people who like her better than me."

"Great," said Stevie. "As ... long ... as ... you ... don't ... have ... issues."

When I got home on Friday, though, Reese was sitting happily — in our room! — working on a model SCUD missile. He gave me this big smile when I walked in. Now, I was really suspicious. Usually Reese only smiles like that when he's pounded someone, but he hadn't been able to beat anyone up since we were grounded. I knew eventually he'd tell me. For Reese, it wasn't a perfect crime unless you told somebody.

Reese finished putting a screaming eagle decal on his missile and turned to me, leaning over the back of his chair.

"Our little problem is taken care of," he said.

I rolled my eyes. This was going to take a while.

"What little problem?"

Reese's face split into a big grin. "The enemy is contained," he said. "She was looking for toilet paper. I told her there were extra rolls in the attic. She went up there, and *good-bye exchange student!* I locked her in. It's just like this movie I saw. You should have seen the guy when they finally let him out of that attic. His fingernails were *this long* and they were black!"

Reese pulled the key out of his drawer and dangled it proudly.

Once again, Reese's plan was flawed. The question was, did I let him get in trouble for locking Camellia in the attic or did I save his butt? Usually, there would be no question. I would let him get in trouble. But these were special circumstances and we had to stick together.

I took the key and went up to the attic.

The attic was dark and old-smelling. There were

boxes everywhere with labels like AUNT HELEN'S CE-RAMIC KITTY COLLECTION and HAL'S VINTAGE HUBCAPS. In one corner I saw a row of potties. I made a mental note of where they were for the next time we needed something to blow up.

Camellia was in the attic, too, looking through one of the boxes. She didn't seem surprised to see me, but then she never was. She was always expecting me before I got there. It was creepy.

"Hi," I said. This was awkward. "Reese says he's sorry he locked you in the attic."

Yeah, right. But I had to say something. I was trying to do a little damage control.

"Yeah, right," said Camellia. "Is this yours?"

Camellia held up a tracing of a hand decorated to look like a turkey. I looked at it closely. As a matter of fact, it was one of mine.

"Where did you get that?" I asked.

"There's a whole book of stuff," Camellia said.

I walked over to the box she was looking in. She was right. There was a whole scrapbook of draw-ings with names scrawled in the corners. Mom must have had every art project we'd all done in school since kindergarten up here. And now Camellia was looking at them.

"So what took you so long?" she said.

I frowned. "What do you mean?"

"Well, I've been waiting for you to come up and let me out."

"How did you know I would?" I asked.

I tried to sound like I didn't care but I really did want to know.

"Easy," Camellia said, pushing her glasses up on her nose. "Reese pulls off this brilliant plan. He has to tell someone or else he can't gloat about it. It's his fatal flaw.

"He can't tell Dewey, because Dewey will tell Lois. So he tells you. Only you're the smart one. You can see that his plan is going to backfire on all of you, so you do the logical thing. You let me out."

Camellia glanced at her watch.

"By my calculations you should have been here three minutes ago."

"Stevie got his wheels stuck in a sewer cover," I said automatically. "I helped him get out."

"That could take about three minutes," she said, nodding.

She was doing it again. She was taking my place in the family. See, I'm the one who sees what's coming next. I used to think it was because I'd been in the middle of my family for so long that I could see it like no one else could. But then this girl comes in and, in less than a week, she's calling the shots better than I am.

I mean, is she psychic? Or is my family really that predictable? And if we're so predictable, how come I haven't been able to figure out what's going on all week?

"Hey, look!" Camellia said. From the way she said it I just knew it was going to be something else embarrassing. She pulled out a boxful of baby clothes. On top was a green homemade bib. On the front of the bib, besides a lot of baby food stains, was a patchwork name done in iron-on decals: FRANCIS.

It was kind of weird to think of Francis wearing it. So I didn't.

Underneath Francis's bib was a red bib. This one had more stains and it was chewed on and it said REESE. Under that — I saw this one coming — there was a blue bib that luckily didn't have anything particularly gross on it. It said MALCOLM. Under that was a yellow bib. I mean, it used to be yellow. Now it was stiff, sticky, and smelled bad. Camellia held it up like a dead fish.

"Dewey's," we both said together. You couldn't really read the name because the W had been eaten off.

Camellia tossed it aside and gasped. She stared into the box like she'd just discovered the Ark of the Covenant in there. You know, like in *Raiders of the Lost Ark*?

"What is this?" she whispered. I leaned closer.

Camellia pulled out a second green bib with CAMELLIA decaled across it.

I felt myself go a little pale. "Oh," I said. "If Francis had been a girl Dad says he would have been named Camellia. Just like you," I added reluctantly.

As I stared, Camellia pulled a second bib out of the box. It was red. Then she pulled out a blue one. Then a shiny clean yellow one. On every bib was spelled the name: CAMELLIA. CAMELLIA. CAMELLIA.

I took a step back with each bib. The blue one was the worst for me, because I knew that one was mine. I had been one chromosome away from wearing that bib. Then I would have been shopping with mom, wearing matching dresses with chopsticks in my hair.

"Wow," said Camellia, holding up the bibs. "It's like this has been my family all along, huh?"

That was crazy, wasn't it?

But I was still thinking about it that night as I sat in the living room with my brothers listening to Mom and Camellia play a duet for French horns.

CHAPTER TEN

That night I dreamed Camellia and I were playing chess for money and I was losing everything. It was a really weird chessboard. All the pieces were people in my family. I kept trying to protect my queen, which was Mom. She stayed in her square and yelled at all the other pieces, telling them where to go. I tried to move Dewey, but he kept sticking to the board. No matter where I told Reese to move, he moved in the opposite direction. Francis just complained that the queen was keeping him from moving the way he wanted to move, and Dad kept wandering off the board entirely.

I lost all my money, and then I realized I'd bet Mom's Mother's Day earrings. Camellia was wearing them dangling from her ears and all I had was the empty box.

Then Reese came in in a tutu. "Dude," said Reese. Then I woke up. I was sweating.

Okay, I know it was just a dream, but the first thing I did was to run over to the end table and pull out the earring box from the drawer. Couldn't hurt to make sure the jaguars were safe. I opened the box. It was empty.

"Reese!" I yelled.

Reese came back into the room from the bathroom. "What?" he said.

"Did you take Mom's earrings?" I asked.

Reese looked at me like he didn't know why I was asking that question, so I knew he hadn't taken them. Then his face changed. I held up the empty box.

"Dewey!" we both yelled together. He didn't come when we called. He wasn't in front of or behind the TV. He was hiding. Reese and I went straight to his secret place. That was a little space under the house.

Reese and I were too big to get into it, but we could grab Dewey by his ankles and pull him out. "Where are they?" Reese demanded. "Cough it up or I'm going to — "

"You'd better hand them over, Dewey," I cut in. "He hasn't beat anybody up in a whole week. He might kill you."

Dewey whimpered on the ground. "I can't. They won't come out!"

Reese and I looked at each other with exasperation.

"Dewey," I said. "Where did you put them?"

Dewey stared at me, then Reese, then me again. He swallowed nervously. I slapped my forehead. "Oh my God, he ate them!" I screamed. "He ate Mom's present!"

Reese looked at Dewey coolly. "Get a knife," he said.

Dewey curled up in a ball. That's what I always told him to do if he was in real danger. I'd taught him well.

"I'm sorry!" Dewey wailed.

"Why did you eat them?" I yelled. I wasn't expecting an answer that made sense, but I did want to know. I don't know why.

"They looked like candy," Dewey said simply.

How do you argue with that? We let him go.

We watched Dewey all day. Every time he went to the bathroom, Reese or I went with him. Mom gave us a couple of funny looks, but as long as Dewey wasn't crying she didn't question it. It was a great way to spend a Saturday. Not.

Okay, anything that goes into Dewey eventually comes out of Dewey. All you have to do is wait. But tonight we were going out to dinner and we needed those earrings for Mom by then. At seven o'clock we were all dressed and ready and they still hadn't made their appearance.

Camellia was there waiting by the door with those stupid chopsticks in her hair. Then I noticed something in her hand. It was a present. You know, this wasn't even her mom. Why was she getting her a present? I know why she was getting her a present, because that's what I was supposed to be doing.

"Let's go," Dad said, ushering Mom through the door. Mom was wearing the dress that matched Camellia's. Dad held the door for Camellia, too. "After you, madame," Dad said. Camellia giggled.

I started to follow them out the door, but Dad let the door go and it shut behind Camellia. I shoved it open again and me, Reese, and Dewey walked out to the car.

"Dewey better produce those earrings before dessert," Reese said. "Or I'm shaking him upside down until they fall out his mouth."

We were eating at this place called Chez Ne Ne. It was really dark like our kitchen is when the overhead light burns out.

"It makes you wonder what they have to hide," Reese said.

"How are you feeling, Dewey?" I asked.

Dewey squeezed his stomach and shook his head.

A guy in a tuxedo came up to us. "*Bien venue,*" he said.

Mom and Dad smiled really politely. So politely that I knew they had no idea what he had said.

"Welcome," the waiter said in English this time. "Welcome to Chez Ne Ne. I am Jean-Luc. I will be your *garçon* — your waiter — for this evening. You have a reservation *pour six*?"

"*Oui,*" Dad said proudly.

We got to the table and sat down. Dad pulled a chair out for Mom. Jean-Luc pulled a chair out for Camellia and said, "You are just as beautiful as your *maman.*"

"As her what?" Reese said.

"He said Camellia's just as beautiful as her mother," I said. "Only he means our mother."

Reese eyed Jean-Luc suspiciously. "I'm watching you," he said to him under his breath.

Jean-Luc pulled out some menus and passed them around.

"I want a Cherry Coke," Dewey announced.

"I want a Sprite," I said.

"Root beer," Reese grunted, squinting at his menu.

Jean-Luc scribbled down our drink orders. "And for de ladies," he said. Maybe it was his accent, but it sounded like he was insulting us. I think we were supposed to let Mom and Camellia order first. I guess it was a French thing.

After everybody had ordered drinks, Jean-Luc left us alone with the menus. We all leaned in really close to the candle in the middle of the table and looked them over. We read the menus for a long time.

Finally, Reese said, "How are we supposed to order? This menu isn't even in English."

"It's French," Mom said. "The language of Ne Ne."

"I have to know what I'm ordering," Reese said. "I might end up with something weird."

Dewey pointed at something on his menu. "I want this," he said to Dad.

"There, you see?" Dad said, taking Dewey's menu. "Dewey's getting into the spirit. He's going to have the *fermé dimanche*."

Camellia giggled.

"Great," I said. "Dewey's going to have a big helping of 'Closed on Sundays.'"

Dad frowned. "Pick something else, son," he said, handing the menu back to Dewey.

Mom looked at her own menu. "It all looks so good," she said. "What's *poulet grillé aux graines de moutarde*?"

"That's grilled chicken with mustard," Camellia said.

"Thank you, Camellia," Mom said. "Hal, did you hear that? Camellia can speak French."

"That's something," Dad said, still puzzling over his own menu.

I gripped my fork. Two could play at that game.

Mom found something else that sounded good. "What's *tête et pieds de veau en gelée*?"

"Calf's head and feet in jelly!" I said loudly before Camellia could answer.

"Thank you, Malcolm," Mom said. "You two are like twins. Peas in a pod!"

Camellia and I glared at each other in the candle-light. We were not like twins. We were two totally dissimilar things in a pod. And I was better.

"Calf's head?" Reese said incredulously. "Do they just bring you a severed head on a plate? If they do, I'm ordering it."

Dewey shifted in his chair. "I have to go to the bath-room."

Reese and I looked at each other. "I'll take him!" we both shouted together.

"Good men," Dad said, thinking we were being nice for Mother's Day. But before we left, I leaned over Dad's shoulder and pointed to his menu. "I'm having this," I said. "Dewey'll have this. Reese will have this. You and Mom should have this."

"What am I having?" Dad asked.

"It's smoked salmon. Your favorite," I said.

"Got it," said Dad. "Go to the bathroom."

With one more quick sneer at Camellia, Reese and I dragged Dewey to the bathroom. We returned defeated ten minutes later. The jaguars were still unrecovered.

We took Dewey to the bathroom three more times during dinner and we made sure his water glass was always full when he emptied it. Once when he moved I could hear his stomach going "bloop bloop." You know, that noise your stomach sometimes makes when you drink a lot? Finally, Jean-Luc just left the pitcher on the table so we could refill Dewey's glass ourselves.

"Do you feel anything?" I asked Dewey as dessert was served.

He shook his head.

"Lois?" Camellia said as Mom was about to start on her chocolate mousse. "I made you something for Mother's Day."

Camellia held out her present. Mom looked at it for a second and then her eyes got all teary. "Camellia, that is so sweet!" she cried.

Reese and I rolled our eyes as Mom opened the present. She took out some bracelet thing. It looked like a fancy shoelace. I relaxed. This wasn't even in the same league as our jaguars. I sat back and waited for Mom's polite thank you.

Instead Mom leaned over and hugged Camellia for way longer than necessary.

"It's a shoelace!" I said to Reese under my breath. I mean, she might as well have made a Macaroni Mom like Dewey had.

"This ends now," said Reese.

The two of us got up and grabbed Dewey by the elbows. "We're going to the bathroom," I said.

"I don't think I'm ready," Dewey said as we took him away.

"You better get ready," Reese hissed.

The bathroom was empty. We took the handicapped stall. All three of us could fit into it. Dewey sat on the toilet with his feet dangling above the floor. Reese and I leaned against the walls with our arms crossed across our chests. Nothing happened.

"Boo!" Reese yelled suddenly.

Dewey and I flinched.

"What was that for?" I asked.

"I'm scaring them out of him," Reese explained.

I rolled my eyes. "Reese, that's what you do for hiccups."

Reese shrugged. "Whatever."

"My feet are falling asleep," Dewey said.

"Kick them against the toilet so they wake up," I said.

Dewey started kicking his feet so his whole body wiggled on the bowl. We didn't get any earrings, but he did fart a lot and I think he did it on purpose. The handicap stall was not big enough for the three of us *and* that smell.

"Come on!" Reese yelled.

"I'm sorry!" whined Dewey.

"Don't yell at him," I said. "You know he can't go when he's nervous."

"I'm sorry, but he's got a small body," said Reese. "How long could it take for two earrings to get from one end to the other?"

Just then the door to the men's room opened. A pair of feet walked up to our stall. Then there was a knock.

"Dewey honey?" Dad said. "You okay, buddy? Your brothers don't have your head stuck in the toilet, do they?"

"No Dad!" Dewey called.

"Maybe I should come in," Dad said.

I opened the door to the stall. Dad took in the scene.

"What did he swallow?" he asked matter-of-factly.

"The jaguars," Reese said. "He ate them some time this morning and we've been waiting all day to get them back."

Dad nodded. "I feel your pain," he said. "But I gotta tell ya, I've been through this before. There's nothing you can do but wait. You can give them to mom when you get them." Dad started to walk out, then his head popped into the stall again. "Oh, and you might not want to tell your mom where they've been."

We dragged Dewey back to the table. We had to drag him because his feet were still asleep. Mom was wearing her shoelace.

"We got you a present, too!" Reese said.

Mom smiled expectantly.

"So where is it?" Camellia asked.

Reese opened his mouth. He looked at Dad. Dad shook his head. Reese looked at me. I shook my head. He looked at Dewey. Dewey smiled.

"It's at home," Reese mumbled, jabbing a spoon into his crème caramel.

"No, it's not," said Dewey.

"Shut up, you little moron. This is all your fault. Mom, we have a present, but Dewey — "

I had to do something. Reese was about to crack. We were going to look like complete idiots — again.

I had a cherry crêpe on my plate. I picked it up flat in my hand and slapped it up into Reese's face. I'd always kind of wanted to do that. There's something really satisfying about putting a pancake in someone's face. It made a wet smacking sound.

Of course Reese didn't thank me for saving our plan. He just peeled the crêpe off his face, licked off some of the cherries, and pitched his crème caramel at my head.

"If you don't want your dessert, I'll eat it!" Dewey said.

At this point Reese and I both lost it. I mean, the only reason I was fighting with Reese was because of Dewey the human garbage disposal. And he wants dessert? I'll give him dessert!

Reese and I both reached out and flipped Dewey's bowl of pudding onto his head.

I'm not sure what happened next. I remember Jean-Luc going by with a tray of tarts, and a lot of whipped cream, and then Jean-Luc yelling in French. Then I remember Mom yelling, "I have had enough of this!"

I looked at Mom. Her new red dress was covered in whipped cream and there was a cherry in her hair. Beside her, Camellia was also covered in whipped cream. They looked just like twins!

Something told me we'd topped last year's exploding eggs.

Nobody said much on the way home. Mom sent us straight to the living room. She unplugged the TV. Reese and I sat on our sofa, staring at the ceiling.

"Well, that was a disaster," I said.

From inside the bathroom, we heard Dewey call. "I got them! I got them! The jaguars came out!"

I guess we should have been happy. But it seemed like too little too late.

The weird thing is, we really tried. I mean, we wanted to give Mom a nice Mother's Day. So how did we end up getting punished - again? Mom didn't have time to really punish us before bedtime so she just took away our pillows and sheets. She said we didn't deserve the luxury. Only good boys got covers, she said. Not only was she mad that we were banned from another restaurant, but we had ruined her dress and we'd ruined Camellia's dress, too.

I think Mom would have really liked the earrings. I can't believe we got shown up by a girl with a shoelace.

CHAPTER ELEVEN

I didn't have any dreams that night. I didn't sleep at all. When the sun came up I got out of bed and went into the kitchen. Nobody else was awake. Francis wasn't allowed to sleep much at his school, so I gave him a call. He was surprised to hear from me so early in the morning.

"Are you getting up early or coming home late?" Francis joked.

I laughed a little, but he could tell I was really bummed out.

"We really did it this time," I told Francis.

"I know the feeling," he said. "That's why I'm talking to you on the hall phone instead of from my room."

If Francis could see our room now, he wouldn't want to be in there.

"What happened?" Francis said.

I told him the whole story. "We had the best present ever for Mom, but then Dewey swallowed it. We tried to get it back at the restaurant because Camellia gave Mom a shoelace that she really liked for some reason. But we couldn't, and then Reese started to panic. And I didn't want Mom to find out where the jaguars really were, so I hit him in the face with a crêpe."

"Sounds reasonable," said Francis.

"Yeah, but then we got into a fight and we got whipped cream all over Mom's new dress."

I heard Francis suck in his breath.

"That's not good," he said. "It was a new dress?"

"Brand new," I said. "She and Camellia bought matching dresses to wear to dinner."

"Really?" said Francis. "That's cute."

"It is not cute!" I yelled. "Why does everyone think Camellia is so great? What did she ever do for you?"

I didn't expect Francis to actually answer, but he did.

"She got me off the hook for the nose thing," he said.

"What?"

"The other day when I talked to Camellia she was telling me that she'd talked to Mom. She told Mom how sorry I was and convinced her that I'd be better off at home this summer where she could keep an eye on me."

I didn't know what to say. *I* was going to convince Mom Francis should come home and she beat me to it. He didn't need me at all. Camellia did it all.

"Malcolm?" Francis said when I was quiet. "What is it you don't like about this girl?"

It was about time somebody asked me.

"Okay, she's completely upset the delicate balance

of this household," I said. "Dewey can't be Dewey, Reese can't be Reese. Mom and Dad are acting like her parents instead of mine. She's better at being me than I am!"

"Malcolm, she can't be better at being you," Francis said. "She's a girl."

"She's a girl who's really good at being me," I said. "It's like this is her family and not mine. Did you know that Mom was going to call us all Camellia if we were girls? I found the bibs in the attic. Camellia's even got her own bib!"

"Malcolm, calm down," said Francis. "I know what the problem is. I went through it myself."

He did?

"You did?"

"I used to be an only child, you know," said Francis. "You know what that's like? You're the center of the universe. Mom and Dad are the planets that revolve around you. And then one day they brought home . . . him."

"Who?" I asked.

"Reese. That bawling, yelling, kicking bundle in a blanket. From that day on, my world turned upside down. Mom and Dad were acting . . . I don't know, like pod people! It was like they liked Reese better than me. 'Oooh, look at Reese! Reese is walking! Reese is talking! Reese is beating up that other baby! Oh, Francis? He's nobody.' Believe me, Malcolm, I'm still working through it."

"Wow," I said. I guess it would be a shock to any-body for Reese to move into their house. "What did you do?"

"What didn't I do?" Francis corrected me. "Let's see. You're not going to tell Mom, are you?"

"It's me, Malcolm!" I said. It was great to have Francis confiding in me again.

"Okay, once we were in the park and when Mom wasn't looking I took Reese out of the stroller and hid him under a bush. I was hoping Mom wouldn't no-tice until we got home, giving someone else plenty of time to find Reese and take him. No such luck."

I laughed. Now that was the Francis I knew.

"I sold him to a kid down the street whose dog had been hit by a car, but his mom made him give Reese back. He wasn't housebroken."

"He still isn't," I said. "When did you stop trying to get rid of him?"

"When I found uses for him," Francis said. "I taught him to swear and make prank phone calls, that sort of thing. Oh, and I taught him to regard all outsiders as the enemy. That was pretty fun."

I listened to everything Francis said. Did I really feel like Camellia was taking my place like Francis had thought Reese was taking his?

"Maybe it is the same thing," I said to Francis. "But what can I do about it? I can't put her under a bush or sell her. I can't have fun with her like you and Reese. She's a girl."

"Malcolm, this is your chance to profit from my experience," said Francis. "Talk to her."

"What?" I said. He had to be kidding.

"I know it sounds crazy," Francis said. "But if you talk to girls, they'll talk back. They're into that. Trust me."

"But why do I even need to talk to her?" I asked. "She's leaving today anyway."

"You need to talk to her," said Francis. "Because if you don't, young master Malcolm, you'll spend the rest of your life thinking that she beat you at your own game."

I wouldn't want to live like that. I decided to do it. Convincing Reese and Dewey to follow Francis's advice was a little harder.

"I'm not going in there," Dewey said. "Did you forget about the killer robot?"

"Would you shut up about the killer robot?" Reese said. "Why should I talk to her? She's the enemy."

You know, Francis really did a number on Reese and the world was going to pay for it. Francis was so cool.

"We're going to apologize to Camellia for ruining her dress. It'll count in our favor when Mom's punishing us for doing it."

Reese looked at me blankly. Apologizing never made much sense to him.

"We're going to show her who's boss," I said.

Reese agreed to that. He loved showing people

who was boss. Dewey was still afraid of Barbie the killer robot, but we didn't give him a choice.

Camellia was awake when we knocked on the door. She was packing. *That was nice.*

"What do you want?" she said.

At first I just stared at her. She looked different. Oh, she didn't have her glasses on. Her eyes looked . . . human. Then she took her glasses off the night table and put them on and her eyes floated out at me again.

"We're sorry about your dress," I said.

Camellia nodded slightly.

"And thanks for talking to Mom about Francis," I added.

Camellia looked at the three of us. "You're welcome," she said. "But I didn't do it for you. I did it for Lois because Lois would be really sad if Francis didn't come home. I know you're only apologizing to me because you know your mom is going to make you."

She was doing it again. Being me.

"Look, I'm sorry about your dress," I said. "But it's not like you said you were sorry for humiliating me in front of my class."

"Well, you didn't apologize for not letting me come to the mall," said Camellia.

"What about what you did to Dewey!" I said.

I pushed Dewey forward. He pushed himself back against me. "Show them the robot! Show them the robot!"

Camellia went over to the desk where the doll body lay under a towel. Camellia flipped the switch and the body started to move. Frankenbarbie sat up and looked around with her blinking red eyes.

"Awesome!" said Reese.

Camellia made the robot stand up and walk toward us. "I designed her myself," she said. "She's not finished yet. I want to give her kung-fu grip as soon as I find a GI Joe to donate it. She's not going to zap you, Dewey. I just said that because you were going to tell on me and get me in trouble."

Dewey went cautiously over to the robot and poked its head with his finger.

"Why did you even ask for an exchange student?" she asked me. "You made it really clear that you didn't want me here."

"It was Mom's idea," Reese clarified. "We didn't know you were going to get us grounded for the whole week. Thanks a lot."

"Grow up, Reese," Camellia said. "Like it's my fault that you got yourself in trouble? You can't face up to anything you do. You're just a big coward!"

Reese did something I've never seen him do before when his honor was insulted. He did nothing. He looked like he really wanted to say something but nothing was coming out.

"And you," Camellia said, turning her floaty eyes at me. "You're just mad because for one week you couldn't see what was coming and guess what everyone was going to do before they did it. Without that you're nobody."

For a second I just stared at her, and then I opened my mouth. "And you . . . " I said. "You do the same thing!"

You're not going to believe this, but that made me feel so much better. I thought she'd figured me out so easily, but it turned out she was just being myself! I mean herself. And she wasn't any better at it than I was.

I saw it hit Camellia, too. Then she ran into the bathroom with Frankenbarbie and slammed the door.

Reese looked at me. "What just happened?" he asked.

"You wouldn't understand," I said.

"We should have known better than to try to talk to a girl," said Reese.

"We gotta talk to her again," I said.

"Are you nuts? She'll just go ballistic."

Dewey walked over to the bathroom door and knocked. "Can the robot come out and play?" he asked.

We heard a muffled no from inside.

I walked over to the door and kneeled down next to Dewey. "Camellia?" I said. "We're really sorry. We really mean it."

I gave Reese a look. He shook his head.

"No way," he said. "She called me a coward."

"You are a coward," I said. "Now say you're sorry."

"I'm sorry," Reese called into the bathroom.

"Camellia?" I said. "Please let us come in. We promise we won't act like idiots. We can do that sometimes."

I heard the bathroom lock slide back and the door opened. Camellia was sitting on the edge of the tub. Frankenbarbie was lounging in the soapdish.

"We didn't mean to ruin your dress," I said. It seemed as good a place as any to start. "See, I was trying to stop Reese from telling Mom what really happened to her present."

"So you really got her a present?" Camellia said. "Lois thinks you forgot."

"See?" I said to Reese and Dewey. "I told you Mom would think we forgot."

Dewey looked down at the floor. "They looked like candy," he said.

"We got her an excellent present," Reese said. He hung back in the doorway, not wanting to get too close. Reese reached into his pocket and pulled out the jaguars. They glittered in the early morning bathroom sun. "Check it out!" he said.

Camellia lifted her head and squinted at the earrings in Reese's hand. Reese took a few steps into the bathroom and handed them to her. Camellia turned them over in her hand.

"They're jaguars," Reese explained.

"They're pretty," Dewey said.

"We took a long time picking them out," I said seriously. "We really want Mom to like them. You seem to be pretty good at knowing what Mom likes. What's your honest opinion as a girl?"

Camellia looked at me and hesitated. "My honest opinion?"

"Yes," I said. "We really want to know."

Reese, Dewey and I leaned forward eagerly.

Camellia sighed. "They're the ugliest earrings I've ever seen."

Camellia winced as she saw all our faces fall.

"When you say ugly," I said. "How ugly do you mean? Like, are they as ugly as a ring of a silver monkey head with a chip in its mouth?"

"I've seen the monkey ring," Camellia said. "These are definitely monkey ugly."

"Oh well," I said. "I guess it's lucky we couldn't give them to her last night. Maybe Camellia can help us pick out something better."

"I know exactly which ones you should get," said Camellia with a smile. "I'm sure your dad will take us to the mall to get them."

Camellia looked at the jaguars in her hand again and laughed. "So what happened last night anyway?" she said. "Why couldn't you give them to Lois at the restaurant?"

"Oh," said Reese casually. "Dewey swallowed them and we had to wait for them to . . . "

"Ewwww!" Camellia yelled.

She dropped the earrings on the floor and jumped up. She ran to the sink and started washing her hands furiously.

Behind her, a grin slowly started to spread across Reese's face. It might have been an accident, but he had finally gotten her back.

CHAPTER TWELVE

"**K**ids! The fried chicken's here!" Dad called from the front door where he was paying the delivery boy. We'd kind of officially agreed to forget about last night and make this our Mother's Day dinner. All through dinner I kept checking my pocket to make sure I had the new present. Camellia had even wrapped it for us, except for the bow, which she let Dewey stick on. Reese always says he'll let Dewey put the bow on, and then at the last minute he slaps it down himself. It's pretty funny.

"Well," said Dad. "This is a pleasant meal."

Left unsaid was that so far nobody was covered in food.

When the last bit of chicken skin hit the plate, Dewey yelled, "We have a present for you, Mom!"

Mom lifted an eyebrow. She still thought we forgot about Mother's Day. She probably thought we were about to give her a gift certificate for a free mammogram, which we did two years ago. We thought it was like a candygram for mothers, but I guess it's not.

"Here you go," I said, handing Mom the present. Her eyes got wide when she looked at it. Not only was it something in a box, but it was wrapped using less than a whole roll of masking tape. Reese grinned proudly.

"Get ready to be seriously rocked," Reese said.

Mom unwrapped the present slowly. I wasn't breathing, and I was pretty sure nobody else was either. Then Mom opened the little jewelry box. For a second she looked like she couldn't believe it. Then she started smiling and crying at the same time.

"Oh my God!" she cried. "You guys, these were just the earrings I wanted. How did you know?"

Camellia didn't say anything at all. The three of us just basked in the glow. Mom got up and gave each one of us a big kiss on the cheek. It was pretty embarrassing but still kind of nice. It was Mother's Day, so she was allowed to do stuff like that.

Mom put the earrings on. They were plain silver squiggles, basically. But Camellia was right. They were the ones Mom really wanted. This was like a whole new concept to me, that just because we thought something was cool, didn't mean that Mom did. It was like she was a separate person or something.

"Hey, gorgeous," Dad said as Mom spun around in her earrings.

"You look beautiful, Lois," Camellia said.

Mom stopped spinning. She looked at Camellia and smiled. I knew she knew how we picked out the earrings. But for some reason it didn't bother me.

"Open Francis's present!" Dewey demanded. If

there were presents in the vicinity, Dewey would make sure they were opened.

"That's right!" Mom said, running over to the other box. She pulled out a present in a plain brown wrapper.

It was something in a frame. Mom looked closely and read it out loud. "This entitles the bearer of this card to one cleansing mud immersion followed by a refreshing kiwi-seaweed rinsing bath with grapefruit toner at Blissful Ignorance Spa!" Mom gasped. "This is a dream, isn't it?" she said. "Any second I'm going to wake up to my usual Mother's Day with the house on fire, useless presents, and somebody bleeding!"

"Nope," said Reese. "It's all true!"

For a moment everything was cool. Then the doorbell rang.

Mom's face fell. "Oh, that must be Camellia's family," she said. We all looked at Camellia. We forgot she had a family of her own. I had to wonder what they were like.

Camellia's stuff was already piled by the door. We all followed Mom to answer it.

The door opened and in walked a man and two girls, one older than Camellia and one younger. The older girl had gray eyes like Camellia, but no glasses. She flipped her hair and smiled at everyone. She had really white teeth. The little girl had a pink headband and was missing one of her front teeth.

"Hi, honey," the man said, giving Camellia a hug. "Did you have a good time?"

Camellia nodded. She opened her mouth to speak, but her sister interrupted.

"I hope she wasn't too much trouble," the older girl said. She sounded like she thought she was Camellia's mother.

"And who are you?" Mom asked.

"Oh, yes," Camellia's father said. He looked like he was having trouble keeping track. "This is Camellia's sister Rosalind, and this is Hyacinth."

The little girl smiled her toothless smile and curtseyed. Dewey curtseyed back.

"Camellia wasn't any trouble at all," Mom said. "We loved having her."

"You're very kind," said Rosalind. But the way she said it you knew she really meant, "It's nice of you to lie."

"Aunt Fern says Camellia will scare all the boys away because she's too smart," Hyacinth announced.

Camellia whispered to me, "Now Hyacinth will tell us about all her boyfriends."

"I have three boyfriends in my class," Hyacinth said. "Jason, Justin, and Jonas. This week I like Jonas best."

"Shut up, Hyacinth," Camellia said. Then to me she added, "Now Rosalind is going to tell me that's not a very nice way for me to talk to my sister."

"Camellia," Rosalind said in that same Mom-voice. "That's not a very nice way to talk to your sister."

This was pretty entertaining.

"I'm waiting," Rosalind said. Camellia scowled. Hyacinth gloated.

Reese surveyed the situation. Then he turned to Rosalind.

"What are you, her mother?" Reese said.

I could see Camellia trying to hide a really big smile. She hadn't predicted that. Rosalind looked as shocked as Reese looked when Camellia called him a coward. It was great.

Reese was standing right behind Camellia to her left. I went and stood at her right. Dewey stood in front of her, facing Hyacinth.

"Camellia," I said. "When you're in town for the science fair, you can stay with us."

"And you can bring your robot!" Dewey said.

Camellia smiled inside the circle of the three of us.

Hyacinth put her hands on her hips. "Aunt Fern says that science fairs are for boys."

"Aunt Fern held a wedding for her cats," Camellia's dad said. "Let's consider all advice from her very carefully."

"I've been saying that for years," said Camellia.

"Well, I guess it's time for us to go," Camellia's dad said. "It's time to make the exchange."

Dewey started yelling. "No! I won't go! I don't want to live with them!"

"What's he talking about?" Rosalind asked.

"Dewey, what are you talking about?" I said.

Dewey just kept shaking his head. "This is my house! I don't want to live anywhere but here!"

Camellia tapped me on the shoulder. "Malcolm," she said. "Did you maybe suggest to Dewey that he was going to be exchanged for me?"

Oh yeah. How could I forget?

Mom gave Reese and me a little smack on the back of our heads. Then she kneeled down in front of Dewey.

"Dewey, you're staying here. I wouldn't exchange any of my boys for anyone."

Reese, Dewey, and I carried Camellia's stuff out to her dad's car.

"Hey, Malcolm," Camellia said when her stuff was in the car. "You've got your family running pretty well."

"Thanks," I said. "So do you."

Reese walked by and punched Camellia in the shoulder as affectionately as he could. She punched him back.

"Later," said Reese, walking into the house.

Dewey had his face pressed up to the window where Frankenbarbie was.

"I'll bring her back to visit," Camellia told him as she got into the car.

"You're not keeping that thing in the seat with us," Rosalind said. "We might get electrocuted."

"Shut up, buttmunch," Camellia snapped. She grinned at me through the window. Reese had taught her well.

"I had a really good time," Camellia said.

The scary thing is I knew she wasn't kidding.

We stood on the curb as Camellia's car pulled away. When they were halfway down the block Hyacinth stuck her head out of the window and yelled to Dewey.

"You smell!" she called.

Dewey waved.

"I think she likes you," I said. Dewey nodded and we went into the house.

"You guys were great," Mom said to all three of us when we got inside. "I'm really proud of you."

"For what?" Reese said.

Mom rolled her eyes. "Hello? For sticking up for Camellia."

"No problem," said Reese as he walked toward the TV. "Those girls needed some serious re-education."

Dewey followed him. I started to follow, but Mom called me back.

"Malcolm," she said. "You were a little freaked out this week, weren't you?"

There was no point lying to Mom about something like this. "You don't know the half of it."

Mom laughed. "I know all of it," she said. "You think I didn't see Camellia trying to get into the middle of this family all week, where you usually are?"

I just stared at her. "You saw that?"

"Of course I saw it," Mom said. "I see everything. And it was very generous of you to make room for her."

Well, maybe Mom didn't see everything.

"Okay, there's one thing I don't understand," I said. "Why is there a pile of girl bibs in the attic that say CAMELLIA, CAMELLIA, CAMELLIA, CAMELLIA?"

"Because there's not much else to do when you're nine months pregnant. Believe me, Malcolm, even when the four of you are driving me crazy, I've never wanted any other children than the ones I have."

Okay, that did make me feel better. Everything was back to normal.

"Mom!" Dewey yelled from the TV room. "Reese is watching a bad movie!"

"Shut up, buttmunch," Reese yelled.

"Reese!" Mom yelled, marching into the room where they were. "Hand over the remote."

"But Mom, it's educational."

"I'll give you an education," Mom threatened, changing the channel and dropping the remote on the couch.

Dad wandered in from the kitchen.

"What's for dinner?" he asked.

"Hal, we just ate dinner," said Mom.

"Right," Dad said.

I stood in the doorway and watched the family scene. Reese was fighting, Dewey was telling, Mom was yelling, and Dad was forgetting things that happened five minutes ago. Everything was in order. It was great to be in the middle again. To prove it, I picked up the remote, changed the channel, and put it down without anyone seeing me. Just as I predicted, Reese hit Dewey, Dewey yelled for Mom, Mom yelled at Reese, and Dad switched to the stock car races. And I made all of it happen.

It was a weird week, but I think it was a good Mother's Day. Everybody came through for Mom. We'd always had trouble with that before. I guess there's a first time for everything.

In a weird way, I think Camellia learned something, too. I don't think she knew how much she could handle before she had to handle us. I think her sisters are in for a big surprise. I sort of wish I could be there to see it.

But as Dewey says, this is my house. I don't want to live anywhere else.

MALCOLM IN THE MIDDLE #5

MALCOLM FOR PRESIDENT

It's election time at Malcolm's school. Kids are being nominated to run for treasurer, secretary, vice president . . . and the biggie, class president. You know the kind. Kids who are confident, bossy, idealistic. Kids with perfect teeth, perfect hair, whose belts match their shoes. Kids who actually like getting up in front of the school and making speeches. Kids who are popular.

Kids who are totally opposite of Malcolm.

So what's up with all the "Vote for Malcolm" signs?

And what exactly *is* the Krelboyne Independent Party?

And, BTW, who told Reese his job was to put the "pain" in the campaign?

Find out in the funniest new *Malcolm in the Middle* book yet, *Malcolm for President*. Here comes your sneak preview!

MALCOLM FOR PRESIDENT

CHAPTER 1

Legislative. Judicial. Executive. If you ask me, the three branches of government are yawn, yawn, and yawn.

I get it. You vote them into office, they make rules called laws. The laws make everyone unhappy. Then you vote new people in because you're unhappy with your first choice and everything repeats.

We're doing government today because the school elections are coming up. That means the hallways will be cluttered with banners. Student candidates who take this way too seriously will be making speeches. And nothing will ever change.

But my fellow Krelboynes are loving every brain-numbing minute of it.

The Krelboynes are a gifted class, which means they're all social misfits. They do math without a calculator, get their homework done weeks ahead of the due date, and actually look *forward* to the annual science fair.

Yes, I'm one of them. But I try not to admit it too often. It's like having a "kick me!" sign permanently taped to your back.

They were getting very involved in the discussion of government.

"It's . . . called . . . checks . . . and . . . balances," my friend Stevie Kenarban wheezed in the time it takes to get pizza delivered.

"The two-party system!" Dabney yelled out with a little two much enthusiasm.

"Democrats and Republicans," Eraserhead offered.

I'm doing my best to keep my eyes open. I'm thinking about my favorite television shows. I'm listing my favorite baseball players in alphabetical order. I'm breaking down the process of oxidation and its effect on a bicycle left out in the rain.

Suddenly, it totally dawns on me. All this talk of elections, Presidents, and government rings a bell. President's Day holiday—day off!

That's the great thing about Presidents and other ancient dead guys. They're always having birthdays and junk like that. Thanks to one of them, this weekend is a total three-day holiday. For the bonus round: Francis is coming home!

Francis is my older brother. My *cooler*, surf-god-looking brother. He's away at military school learning right from wrong and other not-so-fun stuff. But a three-day weekend means he gets to come home for a visit. That is so awesome! Nothing could ruin my day now . . .

"We nominate Malcolm!" Eraserhead shouted out. The whole classroom erupted in cheers and applause.

Nominate me? Nominate me for *what*?

MALCOLM IN THE MIDDLE™

"GOTTA GET ON THE SET" SWEEPSTAKES

Win a trip to see a live taping of *Malcolm in the Middle*! As the Grand Prize winner, you and a friend will be whisked to California where you'll go behind the scenes of FOX's Emmy Award-winning show.

In addition, 50 First Prize winners will be awarded a prize package complete with a *Malcolm in the Middle* backpack, books based on the series, studio shots of the cast, and other surprises.

ENTER TODAY. JUST DEWEY IT!